Sheep in a Jeep

Nancy Shaw

Sheep in a Jeep

Illustrated by Margot Apple

SCHOLASTIC INC.

New York Toronto London Auckland Sydney
Mexico City New Delhi Hong Kong Buenos Aires

ISBN 0-439-18316-2

12 11 10 9   12 13 14/0

Printed in the U.S.A.   40

First Scholastic printing, May 2005

To Allison and Danny
—N.S.

To Sue Sherman
—M.A.

Beep! Beep!

7

Sheep in a jeep

on a hill that's

steep.

Uh-oh!

The jeep won't go.

Sheep leap

to push the jeep.

Sheep shove.

Sheep grunt.

14

Sheep don't think
to look up front.

Jeep goes splash!

Jeep goes thud!

Jeep goes deep
in gooey mud.

Sheep tug.

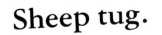

Sheep shrug.

Sheep yelp.

Sheep get help.

Jeep comes out.

Sheep shout.

Sheep cheer.

Oh, dear!

The driver sheep forgets

to steer.

Jeep in a heap.

Sheep weep.

Sheep sweep the heap.

31

Jeep for sale — cheap.